Molly's
in a Mess

Suzy Kline

Molly's
in a Mess

Illustrated by **Diana Cain Bluthenthal**

G. P. Putnam's Sons · New York

Special appreciation to my editor, Anne O'Connell,
who patiently worked with me on this manuscript.

Text copyright © 1999 by Suzy Kline
Illustrations copyright © 1999 by Diana Cain Bluthenthal
All rights reserved. This book, or parts thereof, may not be
reproduced in any form without permission in writing from
the publisher. G. P. Putnam's Sons, a division of
Penguin Putnam Books for Young Readers,
345 Hudson Street, New York, NY 10014.
G. P. Putnam's Sons, Reg. U.S. Pat. & Tm. Off.
Published simultaneously in Canada.
Printed in the United States of America
Book design by Gunta Alexander. Text set in Cheltenham

Library of Congress Cataloging-in-Publication Data
Kline, Suzy. Molly's in a mess/Suzy Kline.
p. cm. Summary: Morty Hill worries that his best friend
Molly Zander will get in trouble at school when a new classmate
tells that Molly is the one who knocked off the principal's toupee.
[1. Schools—Fiction. 2. Friendship—Fiction.] I. Title.
PZ7.K6797Mo 1999 [Fic]—DC21 98-28817 CIP AC ISBN 0-399-23131-5
1 3 5 7 9 10 8 6 4 2
First Impression

Dedicated with all my love

to Rufus

Happy 30th Anniversary! — S. K.

To my MVP's, Vince and Cameron,

and also to Cam's Uncle David,

super hoopster — D. C. B.

Contents

1
Molly Zander

Molly Zander is a third-grader.

She has black braided hair, Band-Aids on her knees or elbows, and brown eyes. When she's not telling the whole truth, her brown eyes get bigger.

I remember the first time I noticed it in kindergarten. We were supposed to bring a "T" thing to class.

Molly forgot.

Did she tell Miss Loo that?

No. She told Miss Loo she had two things that started with T. When I looked at her brown eyes, the little black centers grew like the pancakes Dad pours on our griddle. They went from small to big to *huge!*

I showed my "T" thing first. It was toilet paper.

"I would have brought the toilet," I said, "but it was too heavy."

Miss Loo giggled. "That's funny, Morty."

After other kids shared a golf *tee, tea* bag, Christmas *tinsel, teddy* bear, and *towel,* it was Molly's turn. She pulled up the front of her red sweater and said, "This is my T-shirt." Then she pulled up her T-shirt and said, "This is my tummy."

Everybody laughed but Miss Loo.

Molly had to sit in the quiet chair.

In first grade, the teacher asked us to draw a picture of our whole family. Molly

drew herself playing baseball with her mother and sister in their backyard.

By the time Molly was finished, her eyes had doubled in size. That wasn't her *whole* family. Molly has a father and a brother at home. She was just mad at them because they went to a Wolf Pack hockey game and didn't take her. She doesn't forget things like *that.*

She doesn't forget *anything* about sports. When we're at school, she tosses a Koosh ball in the air or bounces a basketball. She always plays soccer or kickball or baseball at recess. Molly Zander loves sports. I don't mind because I like sports, too. Especially hockey. And when we play hockey in my driveway, she always lets me be the goalie.

Right now, Molly's saving every piece of aluminum foil in sight. Hers, mine, and everybody else's. She's keeping the scraps and adding them to a ball she's making. It's the size of an orange. Molly says when it's April Fool's Day, we can play with it, and when the big kids ask "What's that?" we'll answer, "A silver basketball. APRIL FOILS!"

Even her favorite jokes are about sports.

But the really neat thing about Molly is why we've been friends forever.

Molly Zander knows how to keep a secret.

I can tell her something stupid or crazy or mean or embarrassing, and she won't tell a single solitary soul. And that's exactly how my story starts and ends.

With a secret.

2
My Big Secret

The second Monday in January was a rotten one. The wind was howling all the way to school.

"What's the matter with you, Morty Hill?" Molly said when we got to the upstairs school hall. "You've hardly said one word."

I hung up my winter jacket and gloves. "Promise you won't tell?"

"Of course," Molly said, crossing her heart.

Then she pulled her ear lobes twice.

That was our secret code for "Keep this a secret."

After I whispered the terrible truth, she smiled. "No problem," Molly said. "Keep your baseball cap on."

So I did.

As soon as we stepped into the room, Aya asked me, "How come you're wearing your baseball cap, Morty?"

I didn't say anything. I just snugged my New York Yankees cap down tighter on my head. There was *no way* I was taking it off.

Molly glanced at the agenda on the blackboard. "Haven't you heard of thinking caps?" she asked. "There's a math test today on the geometry chapter."

Aya made a face.

When Molly smiled, her brown eyes grew in circumference. Then we walked over to the frog tank.

"Hey," I said, "there's just twenty-two baby frogs. Where's the twenty-third one?"

Molly looked closely at the surface of the greenish water. "Here he is, floating in the corner. He must have died over the weekend."

Just as Molly got out the long-handled net, Mr. Yarg stopped by. "Another casualty?"

Molly nodded. "Bummer, huh?"

"Bummer," Mr. Yarg repeated. Everybody liked our teacher. He was young, easy to talk to, and made school fun.

"Better take your cap off, Morty. School rule."

"It's his *thinking cap* for the math test today," Aya sneered.

Mr. Yarg chuckled.

"It's not *my* rule," he said. "It's been a North School rule for almost a century. You gotta take it off, Morty."

Molly and I exchanged a quick look then walked into the hall.

While she dumped the dead tadpole in the big sink, I ripped off my baseball cap and flipped up the hood of my sweatshirt.

Fortunately, no one saw me.

Molly tied the strings under my chin and smiled. "Hey, you look like one of those Knights of the Round Table."

I didn't smile. This was a bad day for me.

When Molly and I walked into the class-room, Mr. Yarg was writing the names of the day's leaders on the board. We always had two. They did all the chores. When I saw

Aya's name and mine written in cursive, I shot Molly a look. This was not good.

"Will our leaders start the day for us with the pledge?" Mr. Yarg asked.

Reluctantly, I went to get one of the two flags on the back bookshelf. Aya was there first. She had to get the flag that still had the brass knob at the end. The other knob got knocked off the first week of school, when Molly and I had a friendly duel.

That was the same week Mr. Yarg added another rule—No fencing in class.

I carried the flag to the front of the room like a Marine in a parade. As the kids stood up, Vincenzo raised his hand.

"Mr. Yarg," he said.

"Yes, Vin."

"I think it's disrespectful for Morty to be our class leader. He has a hood on his head. He shouldn't be saying the pledge."

Everyone looked at Mr. Yarg.

I think he knew I had a sensitive problem because he hesitated a long time.

"I'll leave the choice up to you, Morty. Do you want to remove your hood and lead the pledge, or step out in the hall while we say it without you?"

It took me one second to answer. "In the hall."

Molly gave me the thumbs-up sign. At least I didn't have to remove my hood. There was hope for getting through the day.

As I stood in the hallway, I looked in and watched the class say the pledge. Vincenzo was holding my flag.

Suddenly I felt a tap on my shoulder. When I turned around, I saw a woman smiling at me.

"Is there a problem?"

It was Mrs. Devers, our new school counselor. She had introduced herself to our class the first month of school. Sometimes

11

she took Vincenzo out for a chat, when his temper got him into trouble on the playground.

"Want to talk about it?" she asked.

Her eyes were so kind, I found myself nodding yes. She made a quick gesture to Mr. Yarg, then walked me to her office at the end of the hall.

I sat down on the padded folding chair and looked at the walls. There were lots of pictures drawn by kids. Stuff like "I'm happy when the 'Niners win."

That had to be Vincenzo's picture. He was always wearing 49ers T-shirts and talking about the 49ers going to the Super Bowl.

There were also board games.

"Want to play Scrabble?" I asked.

Mrs. Devers smiled. "Not now. Why don't you tell me about your morning?"

I did.

The whole rotten morning.

Mrs. Devers listened, then pulled out her bottom drawer. Man, was there stuff in there!

Yo-yos, Magic Markers, rubber bands, bobby pins, small black combs, hair spray, tablets, gum, Triscuits, and wild fruit Life-savers.

Just to mention a few.

"This should help," she said, reaching back into the drawer.

I looked at the can in her hand. It was mousse.

Slowly, I took off my hood.

She didn't laugh at my four cowlicks. She just put some mousse in my hand and told me to rub it on my scalp.

"I'm having a bad hair day," I moaned. "I wanted to stay home from school, but Mom wouldn't let me."

The mousse felt cool on my head when I ran it back through my hair.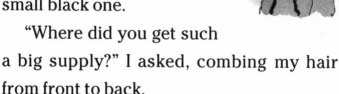

"Here's a comb, Morty," she said, handing me a small black one.

"Where did you get such a big supply?" I asked, combing my hair from front to back.

"The school photographer had forty left over. I figured they might come in handy. So I asked if I could have them. I'm kind of a pack rat."

When she held up a small mirror for me,

I recombed a few hairs into place and thanked her.

Then I returned to class. As soon as Molly saw me, she put up two fingers. That was our code for "You just scored a big two-pointer!"

Everyone stared at me as I walked to my chair.

"Nice 'do," Mr. Yarg said. "Tell me the name of your salon. I want to book an appointment for myself."

"Not telling," I said with a big smile.

Mrs. Devers walked by the room and winked at me. She knew I was one cool third-grader.

3
The New Girl

For a morning warm-up activity, Mr. Yarg passed out a piece of paper with four rows of ovals. "Make something different out of each one," he said. "Be wild! Be creative!"

Molly got to work right away.

Aya watched. When she saw Molly's first oval with a hole in it, she said, "I bet that's an olive!"

Molly shook her head. "It's a deflated kickball. Air's coming out of that hole."

17

Aya rolled her eyes. Then she made a pair of eyes out of her first two ovals.

I decided to get busy.

Ten minutes later, Mr. Yarg stopped by my desk. "What's this one?" he asked, pointing to my drawing.

"A high-heel footprint."

"I love it. What about this one?"

"That's a bald guy on a trapeze."

"Wow," Mr. Yarg replied. "That's really cool, Mort."

I added two other ideas.

A pair of glasses

and a spotlight.

Molly looked over as she tossed her Koosh ball in the air. "Morty's the best artist in the class, and the smartest."

Mr. Yarg caught the Koosh on its way down. "That's a technical, Mol. No Koosh ball in class. You can have it back at three."

Molly put her head down on her desk. She was smoldering.

When I finished my oval paper, I pulled out a maze I was working on. This one was in a castle.

Twenty minutes later, the new girl appeared in the doorway. Mr. Spinoza, our school principal, was standing next to her. "Boys and girls," he said, "welcome our new student, Florence Auchinschloss. She transferred from East School."

Molly and I exchanged a look. That had to be the longest name we knew. I felt sorry for her already. Who could spell five consonants in a row?

Everyone stared at the new girl as Mr. Yarg greeted her, then showed her to a seat at our table. Florence had bushy red hair and green eyes, but when she sat down at our table, I noticed something else.

Her purple backpack.

She didn't take it off or put it on the back of her chair like the rest of us.

"Class," Mr. Yarg said, "why don't we go around the room and introduce ourselves?"

Aya went first. "My name is Aya Starbird. Aya is spelled A-y-a, but you pronounce it *I*, then you add an *A*. My mom is a police officer."

She should have mentioned she asks lots of questions. Aya knew everyone's business,

and soon would know Florence's.

"My name is Vin-cenzo. I'm a 'Niner's fan. They're going to the Super Bowl." Then he made a fist and pumped his arm twice.

"My name is Morty Hill," I said. "I like math, drawing mazes, and playing goalie in hockey."

When it was Molly's turn, Florence looked at the Band-Aids on Molly's elbows and then her long black braids.

"My name is Molly Zander. I love *all kinds* of sports." Then she held up her hand. "I just got this ring. It sparkles like a diamond."

As soon as she said that, her pupils were as big as black pancakes.

I smiled. Molly was fun! That ring was in my cereal box and I was going to throw it away, but she said she wanted it. She said it was a treasure.

Aya stared at the ring on Molly's finger. "It's cubic zircon," she explained.

Molly shot Aya a look.

Aya didn't have much imagination. When I looked at the other ovals on her sheet of paper, they all were Easter eggs. She didn't go out of the lines once.

When everyone had taken a turn, Mr. Yarg asked, "Now, why don't you tell us something about yourself, Flo?"

Flo.

That was a good sign. When Mr. Yarg reduces your name to one syllable, it means he likes you.

Flo didn't say anything.

But a few seconds later, she whispered something. "May I go to the bathroom?"

"Sure," Mr. Yarg said. He always let the girls go.

We tried not to laugh, but it was kind of funny. All we knew about the new girl was that she came from East School, had a tough name to spell, and went to the bathroom.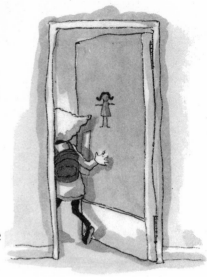

Plus one other thing.

She didn't take off her purple backpack.

"That's weird," Molly whispered to me. "She wears that thing to the bathroom?"

"Yeah," I said. "I wonder why."

Aya raised one finger. That meant "May I go to the bathroom?"

After Mr. Yarg nodded, Aya left the room, too.

She was already investigating the new girl.

4
Blood and Fire

That afternoon, Vincenzo passed out birthday cupcakes. Each one had a nine written on it in red frosting on a brown football.

"I'm nine!" Vincenzo bragged. "Get it? Just like the 'Niners."

"They're the Forty-niners," Aya corrected.

Molly took her little finger and scraped some red frosting off her cupcake. Then she put the red frosting under her right nostril. "Hey, Morty," she joked, "I've got a nosebleed."

After I put up two fingers, I copied her. "Me, too." I giggled.

When Aya looked over at both of us and saw our bloody noses, she made a face. *"Eweyee,"* she groaned.

Molly and I cracked up. It was fun to gross people out. Especially people like Aya, who never did anything crazy.

Molly finally licked the red frosting off her nostril with her tongue. I wiped mine with my sleeve. My tongue doesn't go up that high.

Aya went back to her investigation. "What's that bulge in the medium-sized

pocket of your backpack, Florence?" she asked.

Molly and Vincenzo and I studied the bulge. It was about the size of a toothpaste box.

"Something very important to me," Florence said.

"What is it?" Aya persisted.

"My business," Florence replied.

Vincenzo came to her defense. "There's no rule that says you can't wear your backpack in class, or to the bathroom."

Mr. Right was right.

When it was time for silent reading, Florence pulled out a book called *The Outsiders*. I thought just adults read that.

After we wrote in our journals for thirty minutes, we shared what we wrote. Florence read phrases like *leafless tree* and *coffee-colored murky lake* from her journal.

Then Molly abruptly changed the subject.

"Oh, no! It's starting to snow again. Now we won't get to go outside for recess!"

Mr. Yarg walked over to the window. "Ahhhhh . . ." he murmured. "How would you describe snowflakes, class?"

Obviously, he wanted to keep us in the writing mode. But before anyone could say something, the fire alarm went off.

Bzzzzzzzzzzzzzz!

Bzzzzzzzzzzzzzz!

Molly and I looked out the window. The snow was really coming down!

"Something tells me this is for real," she said. "We don't practice fire drills in the snow."

Mr. Yarg grabbed the attendance book off his desk. "Single file, class, no talking." He was in a serious mode now. There was an edge to his voice.

When we got outside in the hall, Molly grabbed her Rebecca Lobo basketball.

29

"I don't want this to burn up. It was my favorite Christmas gift."

I grabbed my Yankee baseball cap and snugged it down over my head. Wet weather makes my hair frizz up.

Mr. Yarg turned off the light and closed the door. Florence followed at the end of the line with her purple backpack.

What happened next was deadly.

For Molly, Florence, *and* the principal!

5

The Deadly Hook Shot

"This is so unusual," Aya said as we walked outside. "Our school never has a practice drill in snowy weather. This fire has to be for *real!*"

Vincenzo groaned, "And since there's no time for coats during a fire drill, we're freezing our buns off, *for real.*"

When we came to the end of the fence, we stopped walking.

But Molly didn't. Her black braids

bounced up and down as she jogged in place. She hardly ever keeps still.

"Look!" Aya shouted. "There's two fire trucks coming down the street. I told you it was for real."

"Shhhh!" Mr. Yarg scolded. "Quiet lines, please."

I could see the teacher's breath when he shhhhed.

It was *that* cold.

Most of us stood by the fence and shivered as we watched the red shiny trucks whiz by. Their sirens pierced the still air. The snowflakes made everyone's hair turn white.

Except Miss Loo's. Hers was white already.

I noticed her kindergarteners. They were wearing smocks and their hands were gooey green.

We watched the trucks roar onto the snow-laced playground. One by one, the firefighters jumped off and stormed inside the school.

After the last one disappeared into the building, Molly lost interest in the situation and began bouncing her basketball.

"You guys want to see how my sister does a hook shot?" Then she added something for Florence's benefit. "My sister is captain of the Rockville High School girls' basketball team. She averages twenty-three points a game."

"Really?" Florence said. "I've never made a basket before, let alone a hook shot."

"It's easy. Watch," Molly said, moving her right arm up. She meant to fake a shot but actually arched the ball up into the air.

At that same moment, Mr. Spinoza stepped outside to check the lines.

The deadly hook shot continued to travel in one long trajectory.

WHISSSSSSSSSH!

It looked like a direct hit on the principal.

The Rebecca Lobo basketball dropped from the air and landed . . .

Bonk!

. . . on Mr. Spinoza's head!

Everyone watched the ball bounce away.

Then we noticed a furry thing lying on the ground. Was it a baby fox?

Mr. Spinoza looked dazed as he felt his head.

His front hair was missing!

"My hairpiece! My hairpiece!" he mumbled as he looked around and picked up the baby fox.

The students nearby covered their mouths.

Mr. Yarg and Miss Loo exchanged a look.

"Who threw that basketball?" Mr. Spinoza barked as he placed his toupee back on his head.

It was a little crooked.

Molly broke out laughing and quickly turned away.

I sure wasn't laughing. I know what it's like to have a bad hair day.

"I repeat . . . who threw that ball at me?" the principal demanded.

Aya knew, but she wasn't telling. She remembered what had happened to Vincenzo when he told on Molly once. She tied his shoelaces together in a triple knot and he missed the bus.

Vincenzo's lips were sealed.

Then . . . it happened.

Florence stepped out of line and pointed at Molly. "She did."

Whoa, I thought.

The new girl with the purple backpack, the great reader and writer, turned out to be . . . a tattletale.

Vincenzo made the sign of the cross.

"Molly Zander," Mr. Spinoza snapped, "see me in my office immediately after the fire drill."

"It was an . . ." Before I could say "accident," Mr. Spinoza stormed back to the building.

What a mess.

Molly was in big trouble.

And so was . . . Florence.

6

The Principal's Office

Just as Mr. Spinoza got to the school steps, the fire captain appeared in the doorway. After the fire captain had had a few words with the principal, Mr. Spinoza waved his hand in the air.

"BOYS AND GIRLS," he shouted. "THERE IS NO FIRE. WE THINK THE ART TEACHER'S CAN OF FINGER PAINT GOT TOO CLOSE TO

39

THE SMOKE ALARM. PAINT FUMES WILL DO THAT. EVERYONE COME IN! THANK YOU FOR BEING SO COOPERATIVE."

Miss Loo chuckled as she hurried her kindergarteners back into the building.

While we were walking, I whispered to Molly, "It was an accident. It's not fair you got in trouble."

Molly's eyes were filling up with tears. Quickly she wiped them away with the back of her hand. "Thanks, Morty, for trying to help, but I did embarrass the principal."

I watched Molly turn down the first-floor hall to go to the principal's office. She was clinging to her basketball with both arms.

"Mr. Yarg," I called rushing up the stairwell.

"Yes, Morty."

"I saw the whole thing. Molly didn't mean to throw the ball. It was an accident. Can I go tell Mr. Spinoza that?"

Mr. Yarg stopped at the top of the stairs. Then he pointed to my baseball cap. "Better not wear this if you're going to be the star witness. It's a school rule. Besides, Mr. Spinoza is a Red Sox fan."

"Yes, sir!" I said, whipping off my cap. "Thank you, Mr. Yarg."

When I entered the principal's office, I noticed the Norman Rockwell painting on the wall.

It was the one where a girl with a black eye sits on a bench outside a principal's office.

It reminded me of Molly.

All the girl needed was a basketball in her arms.

"Have a seat," Mr. Spinoza said firmly. "Mr. Yarg just buzzed me on the intercom that you were coming down as a key witness."

Key witness?

I thought I was the *star* witness.

Molly looked straight ahead as she rested her chin on her basketball. I sat down in the other big leather chair. When I discovered it swiveled, I turned it around once, then sat respectfully.

"I'm disappointed," Mr. Spinoza said. "Here we are, sitting in my office, talking about fire-drill rules!"

"The wind whisked the ball out of my hands," Molly blurted out. "I couldn't see where it went. There were too many snowflakes in the air. I'm very sorry, Mr. Spinoza, that I hit your . . . head."

"Is that the whole truth?" Mr. Spinoza demanded.

We waited for Molly to reply, but she

didn't. I noticed her black
pupils were the size of
olives.

"Did you think my head was a hoop?"

"No," Molly squeaked.

The principal looked at me. "Maybe I
should change my name to Mr. Hooper."

I didn't laugh.

It was time for me to speak up. "Mr. Spinoza, I saw the whole thing."

"Okay," the principal said. "How did it
happen?"

"Molly was showing the new girl how to
make a hook shot. She lost control of the
ball and it accidentally landed on your
head."

"I see. So, why didn't you tell me *that*
right then and there, Molly Zander?"

"Because . . ."

When she stopped mid-sentence, I finished the story for her. "Because, Mr. Spin-

oza, your toupee was crooked, and Molly was laughing. She didn't want to confess while she was laughing. It would have been rude."

There. That was the *whole* truth.

Molly looked at me like I had just told the world's greatest secret.

Molly squeaked again, "I'm so sorry I laughed."

Mr. Spinoza took a pen off his green blotter and tapped it a few times.

Then he got up and opened his closet. There was a small mirror on the back of the door. It looked like he was checking to see if his toupee was on straight.

The grandfather clock ticked in the background as we waited for his next few words.

"Well," Mr. Spinoza said, closing the closet door, "the whole situation never would have happened if Molly had left her basketball on the rack. We don't bring sports equipment out during a fire drill. It's not a time for basketball practice."

Molly and I both nodded.

"Is it?"

We shook our heads.

The principal leaned on his desk. "Don't make me have to see you again, Molly Zander." He glared at the basketball. "And keep *that* on the shelf until recess time."

"Yes, Mr. Spinoza," Molly said. Her voice seemed back to normal now.

When we got out into the hall, Molly tapped me on the head with her basketball.

"You're the best, Morty. You were so brave to talk about the crooked toupee. I couldn't have done that."

"Sure you could. First you tell the tough parts of the truth, then you apologize. It always makes a difference. Try it next time."

"Maybe," Molly said.

"Well," I replied, "you didn't lose recess, and the whole thing is over with."

"Yeah," Molly said half-heartedly.

"Something still bothering you?" I asked.

"No . . ." she said, gritting her teeth. "Just *someone.*"

I didn't ask who.

I already knew.

7

Bus Surprises

I couldn't believe what happened that day after school. Molly had her basketball under one arm and her Koosh ball in her hand. Mr. Yarg had just returned it to her. We were waiting for the Y-bus bell in our classroom. Molly and I go  to the YMCA every day. This month we were practicing basketball skills.

It was one *huge* surprise to find out

Florence Auchinschloss was *also* going on the Y bus.

"I can't believe it," Molly moaned as she squeezed her Koosh ball. "Miss Tattletale."

When the bell rang twice in a row, we knew our Y bus had arrived, so we headed for the stairwell.

"Ahhh!" a voice screamed. "I'M NOT GOING!"

Molly and I stopped. "That sounds like Florence's voice," I said.

We went to the end of the bus line to check things out. It was Florence, all right. She was holding on to the steel coatrack for dear life, refusing to move.

Mr. Yarg went to get Mrs. Devers.

She hurried out of her little room to talk with Florence.

"I'm NOT GOING!" Florence just shouted again.

When Florence started coughing, Mrs. Devers handed her something.

"She is weird," Aya whispered. "I heard her unzip her backpack when she was in the bathroom this morning. She's got something *very* important in there."

"I don't know why she just doesn't tell us," Molly replied.

"Yeah," I teased, "she should tell the whole truth, like *you* do all the time."

"Well, I have good reasons when I don't!" Molly snapped.

"And she doesn't?" I said.

When Molly lowered her eyebrows, I knew she was thinking about what I said.

The bus driver honked the horn.

Two minutes later, the school secretary came running up the stairs. "We have to move the line. We can't hold the bus any longer."

Mrs. Devers walked toward us. "Morty," she said, "can I speak with you for a minute?"

"Sure," I said, following her.

"Florence is new. She doesn't know anyone. She doesn't want to go to the Y. That's new, too. This is her first time. Can you tell her about some things you do there?"

"Okay," I said, walking over to Florence.

She was still clinging to the steel bars on the coatrack.

"We play all kinds of sports and games at the Y," I said. "It's fun. Today, we're starting basketball."

"I don't like sports," Florence replied as she stared at her sneakers.

"What do you like?" Mrs. Devers asked.

51

"Reading, writing, and mazes."

"Hey," I said, "I have one in my pocket. I just made it today. It's a castle maze. You enter at the moat, and you exit out the turret."

"Neat," Florence said.

Mrs. Devers leaped at the opportunity. "Why don't you sit next to Morty on the bus and try working his maze?"

Florence slowly let go of the coatrack.

It seemed to be working.

Florence and I got in the bus line together, and Mrs. Devers waved as she watched us go down the stairs and out the door.

As soon as we sat down in the bus, Florence offered me a wild fruit Lifesaver.

I knew where she got that.

From Mrs. Devers's bottom drawer.

"Did you know Auchinschloss means castle in German?" Florence said.

"No, I didn't. That's cool."

Molly and Aya sat behind us. I could hear them whispering while Florence tried to figure out my maze. The only words I heard them say clearly were *purple backpack* and *tattletale.*

Suddenly, I got a horrible thought. Were they planning to get even with Florence at the Y?

8

Trouble at the Y

"Gather 'round, kids," the YMCA teacher said. "As you know, our after-school program is not just about sports. It's about having fun."

Molly put two thumbs up. "All right!"

"And teamwork, and good sportsmanship, and getting along with the other players."

Molly made a face as she looked over at Florence. She still had her purple backpack strapped on.

We watched Mr. Williams wheel in a portable blackboard and explain the rules of the game. Florence took out her journal

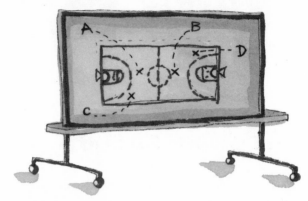

and started taking notes. "I've never played basketball before," she whispered to me.

"It's fun," I whispered back.

"Okay," Mr. Williams said, "we'll have four different stations today. Each one will last twenty minutes. There's the shooting station, dribbling station, passing station, and half-court practice station. There are high school assistants at each station to help you with the the skills. Now, go to one of the four groups."

When everyone made a beeline for the shooting station, the coach said, "Anyone have an idea how we can get into four equal groups?"

Slowly, Florence raised her hand. "I have one," she said. "We could put everyone's name in A-B-C order. The A to H group could shoot first . . ."

"That figures," Molly moaned. "Her name is Auchinschloss."

"Are you related to Herbert Auchinschloss?" Mr. Williams asked. "The principal at East School? You have the same color of hair he does."

"Yes," Florence said. "He's my father. I . . . used to go to that school." When Florence's voice trailed off, Mr. Williams returned to the subject of basketball.

"Go on," Mr. Williams said.

Florence continued, "The I to M group could go to the half-court station, the N to

R group could do the passing station, and the S to Z group could do the dribbling station."

"Great idea," Mr. Williams said. "You are a good organizer, Florence, just like your dad. I used to work with him."

Molly folded her arms. I knew what she was thinking. *Thanks, Florence! Aya and I get to dribble.*

When Florence and I got into the shooting line, I noticed Molly and Aya were glaring at us. They didn't want to miss Florence's first shot for anything.

Florence slowly took the ball from Mr. Williams. She arched it like Molly had showed her, but she threw it up so high, it bonked the ceiling and came crashing down on her foot.

When Florence yelled "OUCH!" Molly fell

to her knees laughing. She was getting even.

"Are you making fun of someone?" Mr. Williams asked.

"Eh . . ." Molly looked at me as she stood up. I knew what she was *thinking*. Was she brave enough?

"Well?" Mr. Williams said.

Everyone turned quiet and waited.

I noticed Molly's eyes right away. They were brown. The black centers were the size of small peas.

Slowly Molly confessed, "I . . . was laughing at the way . . . she shot the ball. It looked funny."

All right!

Molly *was* telling the tough parts of the truth.

"FIVE MINUTES AGAINST THE SIDE WALL FOR BAD SPORTSMANSHIP!" Mr. Williams shouted.

Ooops! She forgot the apology part.

When I looked over again, Molly was leaning against the wall and scowling at Florence.

That was not a good sign.

Florence started wheezing and coughing.

When she asked Mr. Williams to go to the bathroom, he nodded. That's when I saw Molly ask an assistant something. When the assistant nodded, Molly headed for the bathroom, too.

Uh-oh, I thought.

"Mr. Williams," I said. "I have to *go.*"

"You too?"

"It's an emergency," I said, jumping up and down.

It *was.*

But not the kind of emergency Mr. Williams imagined.

"Okay," he grumbled.

I took off for the bathrooms like some bulldog was chasing me. There was no telling what Molly would do now.

9

The Secret of the Backpack

When I got to the basement where the bathrooms are, I stopped. There was no way I was going *inside* the girls' bathroom.

I was just going to be within earshot.

If a fight broke out between Molly Zander and Florence Auchinschloss, I could step in and break it up.

As I peeked around the corner, I could see the sink and three stalls. The one closest to the sink had its door closed. Florence was probably in that one.

Molly didn't see me. Her back was facing me as she washed her hands. After she took a towel and wadded it up, she turned the steel wastepaper basket over and stood on it!

She was getting ready to peek over the stall at Florence! But when she leaned too far, she lost her footing and tumbled to the floor.

CRASH!

Florence came running out of the stall.

She obviously wasn't going to the bathroom because she rushed right out.

I ducked back and listened.

"Are you okay?" Florence asked. "You really tripped over that wastepaper basket."

When Molly didn't say anything, I took another look. Molly was staring at what Florence was holding.

An inhaler. That thing people put in their mouths when they have an asthma attack or get short of breath.

"That's what you keep in your backpack?" Molly asked as she got up off the floor. "An inhaler?"

Florence nodded. "I . . . was supposed to bring it to the nurse but . . . I just felt funny. It's hard for me to do new things."

Florence had just shared her backpack secret.

I rested the back of my head on the wall. Molly was a true friend when it came to keeping secrets. Florence would be finding that out soon.

I turned around and spied some more.

Molly picked up the steel wastepaper basket and set it right. "I go to the nurse lots of times when I scrape my knee or elbow. See my three Band-Aids?" she replied, lifting up her pant legs and then her right sleeve. "Mrs. LeFebre is nice. I can go with you tomorrow, if you want."

"Really?" Florence zipped her inhaler back in her backpack. "You won't tell on me?"

"Not if you promise to go with me tomorrow to the nurse's office," Molly said.

"I promise," Florence replied. Then she added, "I am *very* sorry I tattled on you today."

"You are?"

"Yes, I am. My dad's the principal at East School, and he gets teased a lot. Some kids even call him Bozo because of his red curly hair.

The truth just spilled out of my mouth. I felt sorry for Mr. Spinoza."

"Me, too." Then Molly thought for a moment. "How come you left your Dad's school?"

"He and my mom got a divorce. I live with her now, across town."

"Oh," Molly said. "That's too bad."

"It's okay. Mom tells me I'm adjusting. I get to see Daddy every weekend and sometimes we talk on the phone. I don't blame you for laughing at me in there. It probably did look funny. I stink at sports."

"That's not true," Molly disagreed. "You just haven't played much. If you go to the Y every day, you'll get better."

"You think so?" Florence asked.

"I know so," Molly insisted. "My sister and brother keep telling me that over and over."

Florence reached in the smallest pocket of her purple backpack. "Want my last Lifesaver?"

"Thanks," Molly said, tucking the tiny leftover foil in her jeans pocket. "I didn't apologize for laughing at you because I wasn't sorry at the time. But I feel like it now. You're a nice person, and I embarrassed you in front of everyone. I'm sorry."

When the two of them smiled, I leaned back against the wall again. *Man,* I thought, *Molly got it right this time!*

Just as the girls started to leave, I ducked into the boys' bathroom. *What a narrow escape!* I thought as I rejoined everyone at practice.

Ten minutes later, when Mr. Williams blew his whistle and we changed stations, I had a quick word with Molly.

"What's new?" I asked, acting dumb.

"I'll tell you what's new," Molly shot back. "I just gave Florence a black eye in the bathroom. She had it coming for tattling on me."

I stared at Molly.

Her eyes were getting bigger and darker.

"I *don't think so,*" I said, folding my arms. "I was there. I saw the whole thing. You guys are friends now!"

Molly burst out laughing.

"I know," she said. "I just wanted to see if *you* were going to tell *me* the whole truth."

"You!" I groaned.

After we socked each other in the arms a couple of times, we ran back to practice.

"PLAY BALL!" Molly shouted. Then she smiled as she gave the thumbs-up sign to Florence and me.